Nighttime Is Just Daytime
with Your Eyes Closed

by
MARK LOWRY

Illustrated by Kristen Myers

Our purpose at Howard Publishing is to:

- *Increase faith* in the hearts of growing Christians
- *Inspire holiness* in the lives of believers
- *Instill hope* in the hearts of struggling people everywhere

Because He's coming again!

Nighttime Is Just Daytime with Your Eyes Closed
©1999 Mark Lowry
All rights reserved. Printed in Mexico

Published by Howard Publishing Co., Inc.,
3117 North 7th Street, West Monroe, Louisiana 71291-2227

99 00 01 02 03 04 05 06 07 08   10 9 8 7 6 5 4 3 2 1

Edited by Chrys Howard
Illustrated by Kristen Myers
Digital Enhancement by Tribe Design

Library of Congress Cataloging-in-Publication Data
Lowry, Mark.
    Nighttime is just daytime with your eyes closed / Mark Lowry ; illustrated by Kristen Myers.
        p.   cm. — (The adventures of Piper the Hyper Mouse)
    Summary: A little mouse has trouble sleeping until his father tells him about God's wonderful gift of dreams.
    ISBN 1-58229-076-8
    [1. Mice Fiction. 2. Sleep Fiction. 3. Dreams Fiction. 4. Christian life Fiction. 5. Stories in rhyme.] I. Myers, Kristen, ill. II. Title. III. Series: Lowry, Mark. Adventures of Piper the Hyper Mouse.
PZ8.3.L9556Nh   1999
[E]—dc21   99-40180
                                                     CIP

Down through the valley and just past the trees
Where the red robins ride on a warm summer breeze
And the lilacs and lilies bloom under blue skies
Is a place full of adventure and sweet lullabies.

In a small tiny village, much like your own
Lives Piper the mouse in Piper's mouse home.
And the name of the town? It is none other than Cheddar.
No mouse could have chosen a name any better.

Well, Piper was hyper,
as everyone knows.
Piper was hyper from his
head to his toes—

Even when moonlight and stars came to play
And he had to lie down at the end of the day.

Energy oozed from his every pore,
With a mind full of questions and daydreams and more.
His head would be still, but, oh, how his mind
Would dance through the galaxies, one at a time.

Sleeping was fine
   for the rest of his kin.
He'd hear Grandpa snore
   from his chair in the den.
His brothers and sisters,
   they needed their rest,
And his mom always said,
   "Sleep can rest you the best."

So, Papa told Piper of a land far away,
Where little mice play in the heat of the day.
"Far around the world, clear out of sight,
The sun is still shining, while here it is night.

God knows how you little mice like to play,
So he invented a way to turn night into day."

Piper sat up in bed with his eyes wide open.
This was the very thing for which he'd been hopin'.

Piper told Papa, "How great that would be!
I could jump over rivers or climb up a tree.
If I could go there, wouldn't that be the best?
Then all of you could get plenty of rest."

"I'm speaking of dreamland—you don't want to miss it—
For marv'lous adventures await all who visit.

You can fly over mountains...

or breathe under sea.

Why, you can eat fifty burgers at once if you please."

His mind began filling with possible dreams
His head was now spinning with adventurous schemes
And before very long, before Piper knew it,
He fell fast asleep; there wasn't much to it.

He dreamed a deliciously colorful dream—
Red lollipop treetops and blueberry streams.
Houses of chocolate with frosting on top,
Whose chimneys were stuffed with banana gumdrops.

The air smelled like hot, buttered cinnamon toast,
And the birds sang sweet songs as they winged toward the coast.
The grass at the playground was purple, not green,
And the pond at the park had a bubble machine!

Then Piper decided he wanted to fly;
So he stretched out his arms and aimed toward the sky.
With a jump and a kick, ol' Piper was soaring.
"This is fun," he exclaimed, "and not a bit boring!"

He flew past his schoolyard and over his friends.
He waved to his teacher as he swooped by again.
He decided to fly with his tail all a-curled;
He decided to fly clear around the world.

Past islands, past valleys, past mountains and streams,
He flew past Hawaii—what a wonderful dream!

With the ocean below him, he continued his flight;
He flew out of nighttime right into daylight.

He landed in China; it seemed he'd been hurled
As quick as a blink, clear around the world.
Papa was right; the sun was still shining.
He was startled to hear a mouse who was whining.

"I don't wanna' nap," the little mouse said.
"I know you don't, son, but it's time for bed.
God gave us this time so our bodies can grow
And our minds can remember the things we should know."

Piper wanted to tell him
we all need our rest
And how Mama had said,
"Sleep can rest you the best."
But his eyelids got heavy,
and he nodded his head,
And his hyper heart wished
he was home in his bed.

The sunlight had crept through a hole in the tree. He opened one eye—waiting to see—

Was he still in the air...

...or was he in China?

Was he under his covers...

...or in south Carolina?

But Piper was still at home in his bed.
And somehow his nightcap was still on his head.
And morning had come, another new day.

His family was up; he had something to say.

"I've spent the night dreaming such wonderful dreams.
It felt just like playing, even better, it seems.
I have to admit it. Papa, you're right.
Dreams are a fun way to get through the night."

And just as God created the day,
He created the night in his own special way.
There's a lesson for us, and here's how it goes,
Nighttime is just daytime with your eyes closed.

"The Lord gives sleep to those he loves."
                                    –Psalm 127:2